Happy birthday, Puffin!

Did you know that in 1940 the very first Puffin story book (about a man with broomstick arms called Worzel Gummidge) was published? That's 70 years ago! Since then the little Puffin logo has become one of the most recognized book brands in the world and Puffin has established its place in the hearts of millions.

And in 2010 we are celebrating 70 spectacular years of Puffin and its books! Pocket Money Puffins is a brand-new collection from your favourite authors at a pocket-money price – in a perfect pocket size. We hope you enjoy these exciting stories and we hope you'll join us in celebrating the very best books for children. We may be 70 years old (sounds ancient, doesn't it?) but Puffin has never been so lively and fun.

There really IS a Puffin book for everyone
– discover yours today.

Chris Bradford likes to fly through the air. He has thrown himself over Victoria Falls on a bungee cord, out of an airplane in New Zealand and off a French mountain on a paraglider, but he has always managed to land safely – something he learnt from his martial arts . . .

Chris joined a judo club aged seven where his love of throwing people over his shoulder, punching the air and bowing lots started. Since those early years, he has trained in karate, kickboxing, samurai swordsmanship and has earned his black belt in *taijutsu*, the secret fighting art of the ninja.

Before becoming an author, Chris was a professional musician and songwriter. He's even performed to HRH Queen Elizabeth II (but he suspects she found his band a bit noisy).

Chris lives in a village on the South Downs with his wife, Sarah, and two cats called Tigger and Rhubarb.

To discover more about Chris and the Young Samurai series go to *youngsamurai.com*

Books by Chris Bradford

The Young Samurai series (in reading order)
THE WAY OF THE WARRIOR
THE WAY OF THE SWORD
THE WAY OF THE DRAGON

For World Book Day 2010
THE WAY OF FIRE

VIRTUAL KOMBAT

CHRIS BRADFORD

VIRTUAL KOMBAT

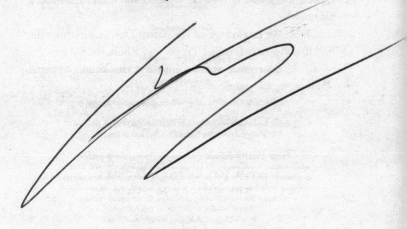

PUFFIN

Warning: Do not attempt any of the techniques described within this book without the supervision of a qualified instructor. These can be highly dangerous moves and result in fatal injuries. The author and publisher take no responsibility for any injuries resulting from attempting these techniques.

PUFFIN BOOKS

Published by the Penguin Group
Penguin Books Ltd, 80 Strand, London WC2R ORL, England
Penguin Group (USA) Inc., 375 Hudson Street, New York, New York 10014, USA
Penguin Group (Canada), 90 Eglinton Avenue East, Suite 700, Toronto, Ontario, Canada M4P 2Y3
(a division of Pearson Penguin Canada Inc.)
Penguin Ireland, 25 St Stephen's Green, Dublin 2, Ireland (a division of Penguin Books Ltd)
Penguin Group (Australia), 250 Camberwell Road, Camberwell, Victoria 3124, Australia
(a division of Pearson Australia Group Pty Ltd)
Penguin Books India Pvt Ltd, 11 Community Centre, Panchsheel Park, New Delhi – 110 017, India
Penguin Group (NZ), 67 Apollo Drive, Rosedale, North Shore 0632, New Zealand
(a division of Pearson New Zealand Ltd)
Penguin Books (South Africa) (Pty) Ltd, 24 Sturdee Avenue, Rosebank,
Johannesburg 2196, South Africa

Penguin Books Ltd, Registered Offices: 80 Strand, London WC2R ORL, England

puffinbooks.com

First published 2010
1

Text copyright © Chris Bradford, 2010
Colour Puffin artwork on cover copyright © Jill McDonald, 1974
All rights reserved

The moral right of the author and illustrator has been asserted

Set in Adobe Caslon 13.75/21pt by by Ellipsis Books Limited, Glasgow
Made and printed in England by Clays Ltd, St Ives plc

British Library Cataloguing in Publication Data
A CIP catalogue record for this book is available from the British Library

ISBN: 978-0-141-33038-9

www.greenpenguin.co.uk

Penguin Books is committed to a sustainable future
for our business, our readers and our planet.
The book in your hands is made from paper
certified by the Forest Stewardship Council.

For Matt,
a loyal friend

Bread

My eyes are glued to the fight.

Thunderbolt has just knocked his opponent's front teeth out. Reeling from the blow, Destroid spits blood. Then, like a bull, the US heavyweight boxer charges at Thunderbolt. An anvil-sized fist lands squarely in the Thai kickboxer's gut. Thunderbolt crumples. Next, an upper hook catches him on the chin. His whole body flips high into the air, before landing in a dazed pile in the centre of the Battle-rena.

The crowd jeer and shout.

I hold my breath. Thunderbolt was favourite to win this match.

Destroid, raising both his fists, slams them together like two massive sledgehammers. It's all over. No one survives Destroid's trademark Killing Strike – the Skullcrusher.

The 3D Streetscreen switches to a red-and-black logo in armoured lettering:

VK

A deep-throated voice growls, 'VIRTUAL KOMBAT. SO REAL IT HURTS.'

An advert comes on. 'SYNAPSE DRINKS SPONSORS VK –' I switch off. It'll only make me want what I can't have.

The fight over, the street kids disperse.

Drifting into the side alleys with the rest of the windblown rubbish that pollutes this city. Unwanted. Ignored. Forgotten.

And I'm one of them.

I lost my parents in the pandemic of 2030. A killer virus. It wiped out millions. Didn't seem to affect kids, though. At one point, scientists thought *we* were the carriers. Some parents even dumped their *own* children. No one wanted us. Now there are thousands of us orphans on the streets.

The whole world went to pot. Then the army took over and martial law brought order to the place. After that, people rarely ventured out. Even though the virus had run its course, the adults were still scared they might catch something. Most escaped life online. That's when VK came on the scene. People needed an outlet – something to funnel all their anger and despair into.

VIRTUAL KOMBAT
THE MOST REALISTIC
FIGHTING GAME EVER!

That's what the ad says anyway. It's *the* Number 1 entertainment show. Everyone either watches or plays.

A *Zing* energy bar hangs in 3D over my head. I turn away. It's torture.

But the massive neon Streetscreens are everywhere in this city. Like sickly suns that never set.

The VK theme – a blast of horns and pounding drums – signals the commercial break over. The logo returns. The voice is back too: 'THE ULTIMATE FIGHTING EXPERIENCE. WHERE EVERY ENEMY HAS A MIND OF ITS OWN.'

Two image-enhanced presenters appear on the screen, flashing their crystal-white teeth. Highlight Time – today's Killing Strikes all analysed in glorious ten-storey-high detail. Heads decapitated, limbs crushed, kombatants killed.

The leaderboard flashes up. Destroid's jumped one place. Thunderbolt's name is eliminated.

VIRTUAL KOMBAT. SO REAL IT HURTS.

The only thing hurting me at the moment is my stomach. I haven't eaten in days. VK's a distraction from the hunger. When the show's on, you don't think about it so much. But afterwards, the clenching emptiness grips once more.

I can't face the reruns and head up a narrow backstreet. There are dumpbins down here, behind the restaurants of the rich and mighty. They still go out. That's if you count sealed MPVs, air-conditioned walkways and dome-malls as outside.

If I'm lucky, I might find a few scraps thrown out by the chefs.

'Hand it over!'

In the darkness up ahead, I see two lads standing over a little girl and boy.

The girl shakes her blonde head, clutching a brown paper bag closer to her chest. The taller of the two lads slaps her hard across the face and snatches the bag from her grasp.

She doesn't cry. The streets are tough. But even from here I can see the red welt of a handprint on her cheek.

'Leave me sis alone,' says the boy, boldly stepping between them. 'Give that back. It's *ours*!'

'Finders keepers, losers weepers,' taunts the other lad. A stocky teen with dark-red hair. He shoves the boy to the ground, laughing as the kid cracks his head on the kerb.

'You won't believe this, Juice,' says the taller lad, his eyes lighting up with pleasure. 'They got bread.'

Street Fighter

My stomach growls. What I'd do for bread.

'Give us a bite, Stick,' demands Juice.

Stick holds the bag out of reach. 'No way!'

'Aw, come on. He won't know if a bit's gone.'

While they're arguing, I creep up behind and grab the bread.

'Oi!' snarls Stick, spinning round in shock. 'That's ours!'

'Finders keepers, losers weepers,' I reply, showing no fear.

Fear's what gets you killed in this city. These two seem like cowards. Bullies. Only picking on small kids. So I'm not scared.

But I'm taking a gamble here. Two against one.

'It wasn't yours to begin with,' I say, glaring at them. 'Now zap off!'

Glancing uncertainly at Stick, Juice backs away. But Stick pulls a broken pipe from his belt.

Looks like I lost the bet.

Stick takes a wild swing at my head. Dropping the bread and instinctively darting forward, I double-block his attack. Then I wrench on his arm, the painful lock forcing him to drop the pipe. Juice pounces on me from behind and tries to strangle me. I elbow him in the ribs. He lets go and I fling him over my shoulder. As he lands, I punch him in the stomach.

Stick pulls the winded Juice to his feet. 'Wait till Shark hears about this. He'll blaze 'n' burn you!'

I stand my ground as they hobble away. Inside, though, I'm screaming *IDIOT!*

Shark's not someone you want to cross. Not even for a bag of bread. He's got a bad rep. But how was I to know? This is Bleeder territory. Those two shouldn't be scouting for food in this zone. They must be new recruits.

Sighing, I reach down to pick up the bag and sway slightly. The effort of the fight has made me light-headed. I need food.

The little girl and boy stare at me, shivering with cold and hunger. The drizzle of rain never stops in this city. Clinging together, it's obvious they're twins. Blond hair. Baby blues. But it's their look of fear and anguish that breaks my heart.

'What're your names?' I ask.

'Mine's Tommy. Me sis is Tammy,' blurts the boy.

As hungry as I am, I hand the little girl back her bag of bread. 'Well, this is yours, Tammy.'

She says nothing, but hugs it to her chest.

'Who are you?' whispers Tommy, his eyes wide in disbelief.

It's a rare thing, kindness on these streets. It's a dumb thing too, I remind myself. I could starve.

'Scott,' I reply.

'Where did you learn to fight like that?'

'*Street Fighter XII.*'

I smile as the memory washes over me.

It's true. Before the virus, I lived in a great home on the south side. My parents were awesome. Got me everything I wanted. The top games console, the latest releases. My dad and I were hooked on *Street Fighter*. I used to try out some of the moves on him for real. Never won, though. He was ex-SAS and a black belt in taekwondo. We trained every day in his *dojang*. One of the reasons I'm still around, when so many others aren't.

Tammy opens the bag, her eyes darting around the alleyway. A mouse ready to flee at the slightest sign of danger.

'Doesn't say much, your sis?'

Tommy shakes his head.

My mouth waters as Tammy pulls out a large hunk of bread. She passes the bag wordlessly to me and shares her portion with Tommy. I look inside. She's left me more than half. I'm too ravenous to even thank her. I devour it.

'This bread's fresh!' I exclaim through a delicious mouthful.

Tommy nods. 'Chef always makes a little extra for us. It has boosters in.'

I savour the nutty taste and moist texture of the booster bread. Already I can feel my strength returning as the energy enhancers do their work.

Finishing it all too soon, I wipe my mouth on my sleeve. 'That was great.'

Tammy smiles for the first time.

Then, just as quickly, it's gone.

'THERE HE IS!'

I spin round. Stick and Juice, fingers pointing accusingly at me, are standing at the end of the alley. This time with the entire Shark gang as backup. In a black leather jacket, Shark himself at its head, his spike of ice-blond hair instantly recognizable. He grins at me. No need to guess how *he* got his name. Two rows of broken teeth glint in the glow of the Streetscreens.

Pulling a pocket Blazer from his jacket, he flicks on its pulse-blade.

It's fight-or-flight time.

I run.

Skyward

Their feet pound after me as I duck down a narrow side street. I know this city zone like the back of my hand and take a cut-through that weaves on to Main. Dodging sleek, bullet-shaped MPVs, I shoot across the road into the opposite alley. But I can't shake them off.

The gang's closing fast. I can hear Shark cursing me.

I have to go skyward.

As I round a corner, I spot what I need.

Leaping on to a dumpbin, I launch myself into the air. My hands catch hold of the lower rung and I haul myself up the ladder. Scaling the fire escape, I reach roof-level twelve floors up. Laid out before me is the neon-lit grid of the city. A vast metal forest of Street-screens, satellite dishes and mobile masts sprouts from rooftops in every direction.

Below, the gang have split. Shark and several others are following me up. The rest scuttle ahead like rats through the warren of backstreets, their necks craned to see me gap-jump to the next roof.

I land and roll. Without stopping, I speed-vault a ventilation shaft and sprint towards the next building. The distance is much greater. I jump anyway, adrenalin and booster bread fuelling my escape. But the drop knocks the breath out of me. I hit the roof hard, slamming into the struts of a Streetscreen.

Above me, the words VINCE POWER – SOCIETY'S SAVIOUR? project out into the night. A handsome, tanned man in a crisp blue suit appears, his silvery-grey hair only adding to his charm. Even without the graphics, I'd have known him. One of the richest and most powerful men in the world. The inventor of VK.

I glance back to see Juice running for the second leap.

He doesn't make it.

Slamming into the roof edge, Juice's face is a mask of horror as he desperately clings on. I think about saving him, but Shark's already across. Ignoring the boy's plight, he tears after me.

I drop down to a lower roof and flee.

Shark stays high and we race side by side on opposite buildings.

He's fast and I have to use all my skill to stay ahead.

Far below in the alleys, I catch snatches of his gang taunting me to fall. Suddenly I lose sight of Shark and I think *he's* fallen.

But then a leather-jacketed figure lands in front of me. My way's blocked. I back off until I hear a thud behind. Stick has caught up too.

My only escape is the building to my right. But the roof's a long way down.

Shark, grinning from ear to ear, pulls out his Blazer.

'Blaze 'n' burn time!'

I've no choice. I *have* to make the leap.

Dashing to the edge, I throw myself into

the void, weightless for a few seconds as I plummet earthwards. I crash on to the asphalt roof, grunting in pain as my foot twists beneath me.

Stick stares across the huge gap in astonishment. They won't be following.

Then a shadow flies through the air and Shark lands next to me. He tumbles head first into a satellite dish. The boy's crazier than I am – and I had no choice!

I limp away, pain shooting up my leg. Opposite me on a Streetscreen the interview's begun.

'Many consider you a great benefactor,' simpers the female presenter, all fluttering eyelashes and cosmetic surgery. 'Not only has your VK program reduced violent crime, but Power Enterprises funds the city's sole orphanage. What drives a man like you?'

Vince Power smiles humbly. 'My philosophy is the greatest good for the greatest number. I offer a way out for these kids. Hope in a hopeless world.'

Shark's back on his feet. He strides over.

I stumble against a mobile mast. Injured – with no way of escape.

There's a sharp *buzz* as his pulse-blade lights up.

'Ain't no hope for you, pretty boy,' snarls Shark, levelling the Blazer to my face.

At that moment, the irresistible melody of an ice-cream van drifts up from below.

Shark hesitates. We both know what that means.

'I'll blaze you later,' he says, snapping off the laser.

Selektor Truck

Hobbling into the square, I see I'm too late.

A mass of street kids crowd a gigantic white truck, the VK logo emblazoned along its side. The tune stops. All the free *Zing* bars have been given out and the PlayPods are full.

I curse. Just my luck. The very night I get stitched, the VK Selektor Truck visits *our* zone!

The truck is the one way off these streets. A mobile VK game station. Prove you're good enough and you become a games tester for Vince Power – winning a place in his orphanage. Food every day, a soft bed, heating, education – a chance at a normal life.

Even if you aren't chosen, each player gets a food pack. That makes all the difference out here – you can eat and trade. Survive.

But I missed out.

Shark didn't. He's settled into the curving black seat of a PlayPod, his NeuroHood already in place. His gang jostle for position in front of his vuescreen. Stick spots me in the crowd.

No point in hanging around. Whether Shark qualifies or not, with a score to settle, his gang will be after me. I'll have to move to a new zone.

Limping away, I hear my name called.

Tommy's sitting in a PlayPod, frantically waving me over.

'Take my place,' he says.

'What?' I exclaim. 'Are you crazy? A chance like this don't come every day.'

Tommy glances at a mute figure standing beside me. 'Can't leave me sis behind, can I?'

He scoots off his seat. 'Saving it for you, anyways.'

'KOMBATANTS READY!' booms a voice through the loudspeaker.

No time to argue. I hurriedly clamber in and pull down the Hoody. Just as the game begins.

Game Over

My brain goes dark.

Tracers of light streak past my eyes and suddenly I'm transported to an exotic Chinese temple. Stone dragons dominate each corner of the chamber, their mouths brimming with fire. Steel spikes stick up from the floorboards in a large ring – the boundary of the fight zone.

This is a single-room Battle-rena, designed for training. No exits. No puzzles. And no enemy or monsters. Just fighter-vs-fighter kombat. An all-out knockdown match where only the survivor wins.

Standing in a circle, the other kombatants await the command to begin.

Flicking my eyes to the right, I quickly inspect my choice of avatar. There's not much left. A sumo wrestler. A female ninja. An old priest. Then I see the familiar white jacket of a taekwondoka. My body morphs from default setting into the lean muscular physique of a martial arts expert.

My avatar's green life-bar flashes up in my lower vision.

It's been a while since I played a video game. Could do with some practice.

VK's changed the gaming experience almost beyond recognition. No more jumping around your living room with a time-lagged motion-controller. Not since Vince Power invented mind-controlled headsets – Hoodies, we call 'em. You simply think your actions and they happen on screen. Then, last year, the sets were upgraded with DNIs: direct neural interfaces. Gamers now *live* the game – in their head!

A blast of horns leads to pounding taiko drums.

'KOMMENCE KOMBAT!'

The Battle-rena turns into a bloody free-for-all. Twenty kids fighting for one place in the orphanage. I glance around, wondering which one is Shark.

A warrior princess is hurled through the air. Blood gushes out of her chest as she's skewered on a floor spike. A muscle-bound

African wrestler hammers a soldier-of-fortune into the ground. Meanwhile, a man in dark shades and a long black leather jacket destroys a Shaolin monk with a lethal combination of flying kicks.

Towering over me, a tattooed Mongol warrior takes a brutal swing with a club. But misses entirely.

A bit of luck. My first opponent's a totally inexperienced gamer. Barely able to control his avatar, he's wide open to attack. I fell the Mongol with a lightning-fast sweep-kick. Then pummel him with a rapid succession of punches – each one hyper-sounded with a gut-churning crunch. His life-bar disintegrates as I finish him off with an axe-kick. The warrior coughs up virtual blood.

Familiar with my avatar's fighting style,

I can react quicker than the others to inflict high-damage blows. I rapidly take out a samurai warrior, a Thai kickboxer *and* the African wrestler, with a devastating sacrifice-throw and arm-break combo.

Adrenalin pumping with the excitement of kombat, I feel my pulse racing. It's like the real thing – but without the pain.

Only a few kombatants left.

Leatherman now advances on me. This one moves with dangerous fluidity. He whirls in the air, spin-kicking me in the jaw. I reel, stars flashing before my eyes. My life-bar flickers and I lose a health point. He follows up with a series of roundhouses and back-kicks. My life-bar drops under the onslaught. It becomes harder and harder to control my avatar.

80% . . . 60% . . . 45% . . . 30% . . .

My vision's now blurred and flashes red. I can't withstand much more damage.

I flip away to safety as an Amazonian warrior attacks Leatherman from behind. She's the only other kombatant left. Until Leatherman jumps up and catches her head between his legs. He breaks her neck with a double-twist.

As I watch him annihilate the Amazonian, I realize something. All Leatherman can do is kick.

Retreating to the edge of the ring, I feign defeat and bait him to finish me. To end the game.

He executes a flying side-kick. At the same time, I drop and slide beneath him. Outwitted, Leatherman can't stop himself and lands on the deadly spikes. Somewhere in the background, beyond the game itself, I'm vaguely aware of cheering.

GAME OVER

My vision goes blank.

I pull off the Hoody, blinking as my eyes adjust to the real world. For a moment, I'm disorientated. Almost feel sick, as if I've been spun round too much.

The crowd's cheering me as Shark's escorted off the truck, his consolation food pack in hand. He doesn't look very consoled. Snatching his leather jacket from Stick, he glares up at me.

'I'll blaze you one day,' he growls.

In his hand, the pulse-blade of his Blazer flashes on and off.

As the truck begins to drive away, I spy Tommy and his sis among the mass of shouting kids. I throw him my food pack.

Grinning, he gives me a good-luck V sign – flipping it sideways into a K.

Kat-Ana

'Welcome to your new home,' says the silver-grey charm that is Vince Power.

He flashes a pearly-white smile. Everyone beams back. It's like a dream for us fifteen new kids gathered in the main hall of Power Orphanage, all fancy nu-deco arches and glass-domed ceilings.

Since arrival, I've had a medical check-up, my first wash in weeks and slept in a proper bed. I've eaten hot food and been given new clothes – an all-black kombat suit with the VK logo in red upon my chest. My name's laser-stitched in white across the back:

SCOTT

I was supposed to choose an avatar tag. But I couldn't think of one at the time.

'You've all shown a natural talent for VK,' explains our saviour. 'You're here to develop those skills and become game testers for the next generation of VK. All I ask in return is that you obey the rules.'

A tall black girl, with the tag VIXEN, puts her hand up. 'What *are* the rules?'

Vince looks at her gravely. Then grins. 'There aren't any.'

Everyone laughs.

'Not in the Battle-rena, at least. But here, the guardians will look after you.'

He indicates a row of thirty or so men and women, sharply attired in red VK uniforms. A large round-faced woman shoots me a friendly wink. The rest appear a bit severe and military for my liking.

'We simply require respect. Don't wander into any restricted areas, for your own safety. Stay within the orphanage. And go to bed at lights out.'

A groan echoes through the hall. Ignoring the protests, Vince sweeps his hand majestically round the refectory, large enough to seat five hundred. 'Here is where you'll eat. Breakfast, lunch and dinner.'

I gasp in astonishment with the other kids. *Three* meals a day!

Above us on the main wall, a huge vuescreen broadcasts the daily VK Grand-Arena show. Destroid's getting airtime again. He's entered the Warrior Top Ten, having just beaten Khaos in a Face-Off. The kung-fu fighter's brains are splattered all over the screen, another victim of the Skullcrusher strike.

'Through the glass doors is the Chill Zone,' explains Vince, noting Destroid's gory victory with an appreciative nod. 'It's the place you can relax after training. Follow me.'

This room's kitted out with sofas, beanbags, vending machines and PlayPods. A bunch of kids are chilling out in one corner. They salute Vince as he enters, but barely give us a glance. Their eyes are glued to a grid of smaller vuescreens on the far wall. Different Battle-renas are being broadcast from the one in the refectory. A digital leaderboard displays kombatants' names that I don't recognize. Even Destroid's missing from the Top Ten.

'Which VK League's this?' I ask.

'Your one,' replies Vince. 'They're feeds from the Training Zone. At any time, you can watch your fellow kombatants fighting.'

On the central screen a female avatar is battling a ninja assassin. She reminds me of a retro Lara Croft, all shorts and tight T-shirt, a samurai sword strapped to her back. The display flashes: GINGER NINJA VS KAT-ANA.

The Ginger Ninja is leaping through the air, executing dynamic twists and lightning kicks. He's so fast I can hardly keep up with him. But Kat-Ana's evading every attack. All of a sudden, she power-drives upwards, catching the flying ninja from below with an eye-watering strike.

Ginger Ninja crumples to the ground. Taking her time, Kat-Ana launches herself and lands a devastating double elbow-strike to the head. The ninja's eyeballs pop out of his skull.

'KILLING STRIKE!'

A fanfare of horns ends the match. The kids in the corner quickly drown it out with a mixture of jeering and shouting. Kat-Ana's name jumps one place on the leaderboard to 9.

'The top-scoring kombatant each week is promoted to Elite Gamer status and goes through to our Special Projects Division,' explains Vince. 'Those who excel in Special Projects then enter the Grand-Arena – a chance to fight for the VK Crown itself.'

Excited whispering spreads among the new arrivals. The Crown is the ultimate prize. Ten million, plus your name in the Warrior Hall of Fame.

Vince leads us down a neon-lit hallway to a door marked TRAINING ZONE. We enter a large circular room. Three men in white VK uniforms are sitting at a central control module, studying banks of mini-vuescreens.

'The Analysts,' Vince announces. 'They assess every fight, give feedback and select your training programmes. By honing your VK skills, you test our games to the limit.'

I gaze in curiosity at the countless doors surrounding us on three levels. All are numbered, apart from a single lower one with a RESTRICTED ACCESS sign.

'Your PlayPods are housed individually,' explains a pasty-faced Analyst. 'That way we can monitor your real *and* virtual self in a controlled environment.'

Door 36 opens with a soft swish. I look over expectantly. A girl with a bob of jet-black hair, a nose-stud and black eyeliner emerges. As she approaches the desk, the tag KAT-ANA is clearly visible on her back. She's kinda cute, but no Lara Croft.

A moment later, a door on level two slides aside. A mop of bright-orange hair blunders out. Beneath it is a tiny boy, his face red, eyes bloodshot.

'That's not fair!' he shouts at Kat-Ana. 'You punched me in the – Oh! Mr Power.'

The Ginger Ninja salutes Vince before stiffly descending the stairs to the central desk. As Kat-Ana finishes her debrief, Vince beckons her over.

'One of our rising stars,' says Vince, laying a hand proudly on her shoulder.

She nods coolly at us.

Vince's blue eyes sparkle roguishly. 'Anyone brave enough to challenge her?'

Pain Threshold

My father's SAS motto was: WHO DARES WINS.

Not one to back down myself, whatever the odds, I step forward.

Door 12 slides open and I clamber into a silver PlayPod.

Vince Power and an Analyst join me in the room.

'What are these for?' I ask as the Analyst straps me into the seat with Velcro restraints.

'This is a second-generation VK system,' the Analyst explains. 'Your brain won't be able to tell what's real and what isn't. Until you're used to VK2, your mind could instruct your *own* body, as well as the avatar's. It's just a precaution.'

Frowning, I look to Vince for reassurance.

'Any problems, press the red ESCAPE button on your avatar's belt,' he says, fixing me with his perfect smile. 'It instantly cuts the connection with the VK server.'

A red scanner passes across my face. The Hoody automatically slips down. A jolt of light combines with a sense of endless falling.

My breath's taken away as a forest bursts into life before my eyes.

The Battle-rena is so vivid. So *real*. I can

hear birds singing and the leaves rustling. Smell the scent of pine trees and spring flowers. Even feel a cool breeze on my face.

It's freaky. Like waking up from a dream.

Looking down, I see the reassuring red pulse of the VK ESCAPE button on my belt. This is the gameworld.

Kat-Ana's waiting for me, her sword slung casually across her back. Close up, her avatar's face looks just like hers. Mine must be the same. Our features scanned on.

'Forgot your shirt, did we?' she asks, strolling over.

Glancing at my chest, I admire my rippling six-pack and toned muscles. I wear loose fighting slacks and black sneakers.

Without warning, Kat-Ana kicks me in the stomach.

I double up, winded. An upper-cut floors me. Searing pain rockets through my skull and I taste blood. In a blind panic, I stab at the ESCAPE button.

The forest shrinks to a tiny dot. Then blinks out.

As the Hoody comes off, I gasp, 'Something's wrong. I felt pain.'

Vince grins knowingly. 'Surely you've seen the advert.'

SO REAL IT HURTS.

I nod numbly.

'*This* is what makes VK2 the most realistic fighting game ever. You experience both the exhilaration *and* the pain of a fight.'

I rub my jaw where I still feel a dull throb.

'Your body's undamaged, but you may experience some after-effects as your brain readjusts,' the Analyst informs me, checking my pulse. 'This soon passes.'

'But I wasn't *actually* punched.'

'With every successful strike, puzzle solved or kill made, the NeuroHood delivers electrical pulses that stimulate the release of endorphins. But get hit yourself and pain receptors are triggered instead.'

'The carrot and the stick!' Vince enthuses. 'This makes for the ultimate gaming experience. Challenges, battles and Face-Offs have real meaning and tension. Winning results in enhanced elation. It's addictive, the gamer never wants to lose – not at any cost.'

'Don't worry,' reassures the Analyst, gently

pushing me back into the seat. 'There's a pre-set Pain Threshold Limiter installed in every program.'

Reluctantly, I allow the Hoody to slip down. I blink and the forest returns.

'Back for more?' Kat-Ana laughs.

She picks a pink flower, sniffs it, then slips the blossom into her avatar's long, brown hair. In a sweet voice, she begins to sing 'London Bridge is falling down, falling down, falling down . . .'

I'm ready this time. Won't be fooled by her softly-softly approach. I drop into fighting guard.

Smiling, Kat-Ana launches herself at me. Her attack is brutal and I have to call on all my taekwondo skills. I palm-block her jab and counter with a backfist. She drives a knee into my gut and I feel a bruising crunch. At the same time, my life-bar flashes 90%.

Kat-Ana attempts a roundhouse kick. I shin-block it and drop into a spinning sweep-kick. I catch her by the ankles, knocking her to the ground. A euphoric rush floods my body as Kat-Ana loses 20% of her life-bar.

'You got skills for a newbie,' admits Kat-Ana, flipping back to her feet. 'But it won't save you.'

She drives into me. I buckle under her onslaught. 75%. Pain flares round my body as she lands strike after strike. 60%. I manage to counter and force her to retreat across the fight zone. Even manage to land a few hits myself. Endorphins wipe out the pain. But she's too fast for me.

Slipping to my outside, Kat-Ana roundhouse

kicks me. 45%. A kidney punch then drops me to my knees. 35%.

Before I can recover, Kat-Ana unsheathes her sword.

'NO!' I cry.

But it's too late. She slices off my head.

'KILLING STRIKE!'

I scream as white noise rips through me.

Then nothing. I'm back in the real world.

'Hmm ... Not bad,' says Vince as I emerge out of Door 12, dazed and rubbing my neck. 'New kombatants rarely survive more than a few seconds.'

To my mind it felt like seconds. But the digi-clock on the wall shows a plug-in time of over five minutes.

A bell rings. 'That'll be lunch. This is where I say goodbye.'

We salute Vince, and two guardians escort us back to the refectory. The place is crammed with kid kombatants. I spot Kat-Ana in the queue and go up to her.

'No need to cut my head off!' I protest, still feeling a hot itch where the blade went through my virtual neck.

'Don't be such a sore loser,' she replies, passing me a tray. 'It's just a game. Anyway, with a face like yours, I was doing you a favour!'

Before I can think of a comeback she says, 'You should try the syn-fish,' then blows me a kiss and walks away. 'Tastes like the real thing.'

The Catch

'Here you are, luv,' says the friendly guardian, smiling broadly as she dumps an extra helping of syn-fish on my plate. 'Looks like you could do with building up.'

I thank her and wander round the hall looking for a seat. The Ginger Ninja sees me and slides along his bench to make space. I take the invite.

'I hear Kat-Ana gave you a haircut!' he

sniggers, slurping at his cherry-flavoured Synapse.

'At least my eyeballs stayed in my head,' I shoot back.

Ginger Ninja laughs, rubbing his still-bloodshot eyes.

'So how come she's got a weapon?' I ask quietly, nodding at Kat-Ana on the other side of our table.

'It's a Mod,' he replies. 'The more training sessions you do and Face-Offs you win, the more experience points you earn. With 'em you can purchase Mods and Power-Ups in the game. A samurai sword doesn't come cheap, though. A *lot* of gameplay required.'

'What other gear can you get?'

Ginger Ninja grins devilishly. 'Whatever your wicked heart desires! Got meself a set of exploding throwing stars. They do *serious* damage. I'll show you if you're up for a Face-Off.'

'Sounds tempting,' I say. Though I'm not so sure I want to experience my body parts being blown off, VK-style.

Ginger Ninja cranes round to look at my tag.

'What sort of avatar name is Scott, anyways?'

'It's *my* name,' I reply, suddenly wishing I'd thought of a decent tag.

Kat-Ana looks up. 'It's good to keep a handle on reality. Spend too long in the game and you soon forget what's real.'

'So what's your name?'

She smiles at me. 'Kate.'

I turn to the Ginger Ninja. 'And yours?'

'I need no other name,' replies Ginger Ninja, pointing at his carrot top then executing a karate chop in mid-air.

Kate rolls her eyes. 'See what I mean? Bet he doesn't even remember.'

Ginger Ninja ignores her and takes another slurp of Synapse.

'So, Kate, what's the deal here?' I ask. 'Test a few games and we get fed and housed?'

'Pretty much.'

I look round at the hundreds of other kids tucking into their food. 'All this seems too good to be true. What's the catch?'

'Haven't found it yet.'

'But why so *many* testers?'

'Who cares?' says Ginger Ninja, forking more syn-fish into his mouth. 'As long as I'm fed, I'll play. It beats the streets any day.'

Kate picks up her tray. 'I'll show you where to dump this.'

I follow her to the recycling zone.

Glancing round, Kate waits for a stern-faced guardian to pass by. Then, leaning in close, whispers, 'There *is* a catch. VK's addictive. Dangerously so.'

'So why are you still playing?' I ask, all of a sudden getting the feeling we're being watched.

'You've got to play the game to get out.'

As the guardian strides over, Kate drops her tray down the chute.

'My advice. Never forget who you are.'

Trigger Time

The Analyst wordlessly hands me my training report.

Performance: 5 out of 10.

Bruiser, a Brazilian capoeira fighter, destroyed me in the last Face-Off. My back still aches from where he power-kicked me.

After two months of gameplay, I've climbed into the upper ranks of the League. But now I'm struggling to keep my position. Even with a Mod and a Power-Up. A pair of Kevlar armguards that block any blade. And a single-use Mega-Punch – trebling the damage I inflict for one strike.

Not that it helped much against Bruiser. Like Kat-Ana, he moves too fast for me to land it.

'What's up?' asks Ginger Ninja as I enter the Chill Zone and flop on a beanbag next to him and Kate.

'However hard I try, I keep getting beat to the Killing Strike,' I admit.

Kate looks up from her avatar fashion e-mag. 'Your skills are good,' she says. 'But you need to master Trigger Time.'

I frown at her. 'That's not in my feedback.'

'That's cos the Analysts don't know about it. It's not an official technique.

Come on, I'll show you.'

'Hey, you promised to teach *me*!' complains Ginger Ninja.

'You're not ready for it,' replies Kate, heading for the door.

My body protests at leaving the beanbag. Gaming for three hours straight, my brain aches like a strained muscle. VK's a serious workout. Your mind *believes* the body's done all that fighting. By the end of the first week, it felt like I'd run a marathon then been mashed by a runaway MPV.

Even now I'm brain-fit, VK's still a drain. But I *can't* resist. I'm hooked.

We enter the Training Zone. No Analysts at the control module.

'Downtime,' explains Kate. 'We can still log on, though.'

She presses a touchscreen and two PlayPod doors open.

'What's behind here?' I ask, checking out the restricted-access door.

'The guardians don't like it when you snoop around.'

'It might lead outside.'

'Curiosity killed the rat,' she says as I try the handle.

'You mean, cat.'

'Cat, rat, whatever,' she says. 'When you VK loads, words get jumbled up.'

'It's locked anyway.'

We clamber into our PlayPods and boot up.

A shooting-range Battle-rena blinks into life, complete with armoury. Kat-Ana's standing beside me.

'Take this,' she says, passing me a handgun.

Kat-Ana walks to the end of the range. 'Shoot me.'

I hesitantly raise the gun. I know it's only virtual, but it feels wrong.

'Won't it hurt pretty bad?'

'Do it!'

I pull the trigger. BANG. With lightning speed, Kat-Ana bends to one side, her body flickering as the bullet penetrates the target behind.

'But that's impossible!'

'Not in VK. This is a computer-generated world implanted in your head. It's only impossible because that's what you believe.'

Kat-Ana hands me a suit of Kevlar armour. 'Put this on, or else you'll feel beat up when we finish.'

'You're going to shoot *me*?'

She nods. 'To master Trigger Time, your brain has to function quicker than the game can download into your head.'

'Sounds tricky,' I reply as Kat-Ana makes me stand before the target.

'It is. But by concentrating hard enough, you can bend the rules of the game. Slow down virtual time.'

She takes aim at me. 'Think of it like intense meditation. Focus on the gun, my every movement. See it all. Even before it happens.'

I'm sweating now. The barrel pointed at my chest. 'But how will I know if I'm getting it right?'

'Your opponent appears to attack in slow-mo. But you don't. That's when you can evade or land any strike.'

She fires.

I don't even see the bullet. But I feel the heavy slug impact against my chest. I get blown off my feet.

'Concentrate!' says Kat-Ana, reloading.

Rubbing my bruised ribs, I get back up and focus on her movements. Kat-Ana raises the gun and takes aim. She seems slower this time. But that could be my imagination.

BANG. Like a battering-ram, the bullet catches my side and spins me round.

'Better,' she says. 'At least you moved this time.'

The pain makes me even more determined. I centre my mind on her. Breaking down her every movement. Hand rising. Finger on trigger. Squeezing of muscle. Click of ignition. Flare of barrel. A low, long, rumbling bang.

The bullet exiting. Flying through the air. I shift to one side. Watch the slug pass me by. Pierce the target.

Like a thunderclap, time catches up. Sound and vision compressing back to normality.

'Congratulations!' calls Kat-Ana. 'Now you've done it once, the technique will be much easier next time.'

Kat-Ana presses her ESCAPE button and disappears.

The Battle-rena blinks out.

As we head back to dinner, I ask, 'It's a neat trick, but what if everyone's using Trigger Time?'

'You can't keep it up for more than a few seconds. Creates too much brain strain. So pick your moments.'

'But now I know it, aren't you worried I'll beat you?'

'You won't get the chance,' replies Kate, grinning. 'I'm one Face-Off from becoming an Elite Gamer. When I win, I'll be top of the League. Then I'm out of here. Special Projects! VK for real. The Crown. Fame and fortune, baby. Fame and fortune.'

My mouth drops open.

Standing in the refectory queue is Shark.

Blaze 'n' Burn

I'm backed into a corner.

Shark advances on me, fists raised. I dodge the jab. Counter with a hook punch. His head rocks with the blow but he keeps up his attack, kneeing me in the stomach.

Gasping for breath, I barely avoid his axe-kick. His heel passes my head and slams into the floor, shattering the tiles.

I kick him hard in the chest. He flies backwards into the wall. Giving him no time to recover, I bear down on him. Determined to finish the fight.

From out of nowhere, Shark pulls a Blazer.

'Blaze 'n' burn time!' he sneers.

The pulse-blade slashes across my chest. I jump back, but its laser edge rips through my skin. Crimson splashes of red streak the floor as blood pours from the wound.

Gloating, Shark then rams the Blazer into me. I try to block, but it's too late. I feel the burn as the pulse-blade enters my stomach and grimace in pain as he twists it.

'That's for making me suffer another two months on those stinking streets!'

Pulling the pulse-blade out, I can only watch as he goes for the Killing Strike.

He raises the Blazer, his face contorted

with fury. The pulse-blade glows orange in the eco-light, its laser arcing towards my neck.

Concentrating hard, I see it all in slow-mo.

With the last of my energy, I roll to the side, Power Up and use my Mega-Punch. My fist catches him square on the temple. His eyes spin in his head like a slot machine. I've hit the jackpot.

'KILLING STRIKE!' booms the VK ringmaster.

The Battle-rena shrinks to a dot and blinks out.

Emerging from my PlayPod, my stomach throbs where the virtual blade cut into me. But it soon fades beneath the glorious high of my win. I also buzz from my first kombat use of Trigger Time. It's taken me two weeks of constant practice to perfect it.

Shark exits, holding his head in his hands. The loser. No addictive kick of endorphins for him.

As we approach the Analysts for our feedback, he narrows his eyes and spits in my face.

'I don't know *how* you beat me. But I'll blaze you for *real* one of these days.'

Missing In Action

'Have you seen Kate?' I ask.

Ginger Ninja barely looks away from the refectory's vuescreen. It's VK Primetime. Destroid's climbed another place. And to my dismay, he's just annihilated the Korean taekwondo fighter, Spider.

'Nah,' says Ginger Ninja, stuffing a *Zing* bar into his mouth. 'Not since she went training for tomorrow's Face-Off.'

I head down to the Training Zone, but

she's not plugged in. Must have got an early night.

Kate's still not around at breakfast. That worries me. I check out the dorms, the Training Zone and lastly the Chill Zone.

'Anyone seen Kate?'

I'm met with blank looks.

'Kat-Ana?' I repeat, irritated with their indifference.

Shark flashes his razor grin at me. 'Lost your girlfriend?'

'She's not my girlfriend,' I snap. 'What you got to smile about anyway?'

'Nothing,' replies Shark, a sly look in his eyes.

'I think Kat-Ana qualified as an Elite Gamer,' pipes up Vixen, pointing to the leaderboard.

Kate's tag is no longer listed.

'Did you see the final Face-Off?'

Vixen shakes her head.

'Who fought her? Did *anyone* see it?'

I'm greeted with apathetic silence. Kate's missing in action and no one cares. They're all too zoned-out with VK. Granted, a lot of kid kombatants pass through the system. But something's wrong here. Final Face-Offs always draw a crowd in the Chill Zone.

'Won't she have gone to Special Projects?' suggests Vixen.

'But she'd have told me.'

'That's girls for you!' tuts Ginger Ninja, rolling his eyes.

The guardians' sole response to my questioning about Kat-Ana's sudden disappearance is 'Qualified'. Even the friendly one in the kitchen was no help.

Maybe I'm being paranoid. I just thought we were friends. That she'd at least say goodbye.

Watching VK Primetime over the following days, I keep a hopeful eye out for Kat-Ana in the Grand-Arena League. But her tag doesn't appear.

'Hey, Scott,' whispers Vixen as we line up for dinner a week later. 'I hear Shark has it in for you.'

I nod cautiously.

'Rumour is, he's somehow got himself a Blazer. I'd watch your back.'

I park myself beside Ginger Ninja, but no longer feel like eating. Shark's sitting three tables over, carving his syn-beef and veg.

Blaze 'n' burn.

It's only a matter of time. I can't avoid him forever.

I have to get out.

But how? The guardians ensure *no one* leaves the building.

The orphanage is starting to feel more like a prison than a sanctuary.

Kate said the only way out is through the game. Seems, for the second time, my very life depends upon it.

Elite Gamer

'Congratulations,' says the Analyst without enthusiasm. 'Top of the League. You've qualified as an Elite Gamer.'

I want to jump for joy. But I'm too exhausted.

Three weeks of solid VK has paid off, though. I'm going through to Special Projects. Maybe I'll find out what happened to Kate.

Whatever, it's a relief after playing cat-and-mouse with Shark every day. Avoiding him at all costs. Training every hour. Sticking to the crowded refectory and Chill Zone. Never alone. Though I'm not in his dorm, even at night I have to keep sharp.

Hard going, when my brain's so mashed with gameplay I can barely remember who I am.

I head to the showers to freshen up before dinner.

As I'm getting changed into a clean kombat suit, I hear an ominous buzz. The orange glow of a pulsating Blazer reflects off the lockers.

Glancing round, I find the changing room's suddenly deserted.

Then Shark appears.

'No more games,' he hisses. 'This blazing's for *real*.'

I back towards the showers. There's only one way out. And Shark's between me and the exit.

Grabbing my towel, I wrap it round my hand. It may give me a precious second or two to disarm him, before the pulse-blade burns through my fingers.

Shark goes to blaze me, when a *swoosh* alerts us to an opening door. Hurriedly switching off the Blazer, he pockets the weapon.

'Scott!' barks a guardian. 'Special Projects. Follow me.'

I push past Shark, who's silently fuming. He's missed his final opportunity to blaze 'n' burn me.

I'm out of here.

As I'm led down the corridor, I spot Vixen

in the Chill Zone and give her a wave. I've no one else to say goodbye to. Without Kat-Ana in the League, Ginger Ninja finally qualified as an Elite Gamer the week before, defeating Bruiser in his last Face-Off.

The guardian leads me into the Training Zone.

Door 1 is open, the PlayPod primed, an Analyst by its side.

'Is this Special Projects?' I ask, somewhat confused as he gets ready to plug me in.

The Analyst nods and straps me down.

'But isn't it at a different site?'

I'm concerned Shark might get another chance to blaze me.

'Don't worry,' says the Analyst. 'You're not coming back.'

Before I can protest, the Hoody slips down.

A jolt of light. A gliding sensation.

I boot into a ferocious Battle-rena.

No Escape

The castle courtyard is overrun with kombatants. Fighting tooth and nail against one another, blood flowing across the stone cobbles. It's carnage.

Multiplayer kombat. Just like Primetime VK, where players plug in from around the world to fight for the Crown.

A samurai swordsman charges at me.

I block his *katana* blade with my armguard. Then front-kick him in the chest. As he clambers to his feet, I catch him with a spinning hook-kick across the jaw. He makes a desperate swing with his sword, but my vertical fist punch to the head finishes him off. His life-bar blinks out.

The victory gives me a much-needed boost.

Then a fearsome Maori warrior jumps from the battlements, roaring. His face is a swirl of black tattoos and, in his hand, he carries a great barbed spear.

His roaring battle chant sends a chill through my body.

Pounding his chest and snarling at me, he advances.

I power-kick him in the gut, but it has zero effect. A great slab of a fist smashes me in the face, breaking my nose. My life-bar reads 80%.

My head rings with pain and my vision flashes red.

The warrior knees me hard in the side. I feel a rib crack. Pain shooting through me. 65%.

Stumbling over the samurai's lifeless body, I fall to the ground. The Maori warrior drives his spear into my stomach. I scream. The agony's overpowering.

What's happened to the Pain Threshold Limiter? The game *never* felt this bad before. Never this *real*.

My life-bar drops to 50%.

It's like I'm dying. 45%.

I stab furiously at the ESCAPE button on my belt. 40%.

Nothing happens.

The pain intensifies as the warrior pulls out the spear. 35%.

In a last desperate attempt, I crawl away.

But the Maori warrior grabs me by my ankle and flings me into the castle wall. 25%.

The pain rises in my head, like a searing fireball.

I'm losing consciousness, still feebly pressing the button.

The Maori warrior roars at me, raising his spear to deliver the Killing Strike.

But a kombatant in shorts and T-shirt jumps between us. Her samurai sword slices through him. The spear drops to the floor, hands still attached. The warrior's life-bar flickers critical before Kat-Ana finishes him off.

Sheathing her sword, she begins to sing. 'London Bridge is falling down, falling down, falling down . . .'

My vision pixelates, breaking apart as the signal corrupts.

Kat-Ana slaps me hard in the face. 'Stay with me.'

'What did you do that for?' I mumble, confused and swimming in pain.

'You need to focus on being alive. And stop moaning. It's only a virtual slap!'

Kat-Ana hauls me to my feet.

'We've got to get out of here,' she says, dragging me in the direction of the drawbridge. 'And stop pressing that stupid button. There is *no* escape.'

Reality Check

'There has to be some mistake,' I gasp as Kat-Ana lays me gently on the floor of a cave.

She hands me a health pack. My wound heals in seconds, my life-bar regenerating to 75%.

'No mistake,' she replies. 'We're plugged into the Grand-Arena.'

I stare at her, stunned. The official fighting world of VK2! A series of interconnected

Battle-renas where kombatants have to fight their way through to the Crown.

'But I was entering Special Projects. I shouldn't be here.'

'None of us should.'

'You mean there are others?'

Kat-Ana nods.

I sit up, my head throbbing. 'It feels as if my brain's been fried.'

'It has. You almost died back there,' she points out.

'But this is just a *game*!'

'No. This is reality,' Kat-Ana insists.

'I don't understand.'

'Yesterday, when I left you to go training –'

'Kate, you've been gone four weeks,' I interrupt.

Her mouth drops open in shock. 'You lose

all track of time in VK,' she explains, slumping down next to me.

A far-away look enters her eyes and she begins to hum 'London Bridge' again.

'Are you all right?' I ask.

Kat-Ana snaps out of her daze. 'Sorry. Anyways, I headed to the Training Zone. The restricted-access door was open. I saw a boy being wheeled past on a stretcher. The top of his head was black and smoking. The Analysts said the DNIs were too powerful. The second "Burn Out" that week.'

A cold chill runs through my body at her words.

'The VK2 program demands too much,' she adds. 'Our brains blow like a fuse.'

'Are you saying if we die in the Grand-Arena, we die in the *real* world too?'

'Apparently so.'

'But why didn't you tell anyone?'

She smiles apologetically. 'I tried to, but they sealed the doors before I could escape. Strapped me into the PlayPod. The next thing I knew I was fighting for my life in the Grand-Arena, the ESCAPE button disabled.'

I punch the wall in anger. 'So we're just lab rats for Vince Power!'

'Pretty much. But we're not only testing the game, we *are* the game.'

'What?'

'You know the advert: WHERE EVERY ENEMY HAS A MIND OF ITS OWN.'

I nod slowly, not wanting to believe what she's about to tell me.

'Well, *we're* the enemy, Scott. That's why

Vince Power needs so many kids to feed his system. And now we're part of the game, *every* VK2 player in the world is out to kill us!'

Back Door

'We must keep moving,' says Kat-Ana, anxiously peering over her shoulder.

I follow her gaze down the long deserted road behind us.

'Why?' I ask, taking a rest upon a rock. My stomach's still sore from the attack.

'VK2 will send Skirmishers. Electro-bots to drive us towards the next Battle-rena. We need to avoid trouble until your life-bar fully regenerates. You'll need *all* of it, if you're gonna survive.'

My bar pulses green. 89%. 'Give me a minute.'

Reluctantly, Kat-Ana sits down next to me. She starts singing again. 'London Bridge is falling down, falling down . . .'

'What's with the nursery rhyme?'

She stops and blinks, as if she's forgotten where she is. 'It keeps me connected to the real world. Reminds me of my dad. He used to sing it to me as a child.'

Tears run down Kat-Ana's face. 'It's the only thing that keeps me going,' she sobs.

It's strange to see a tough warrior princess crying. But I know that behind the avatar lies the real Kate. I put my arm tentatively round her. Hoping it's some comfort.

'Most kid kombatants you meet in VK2 have forgotten who they are,' she says, wiping her eyes. 'The game's taken over their minds. There is no other world to them.'

The thought of becoming lost forever in VK sends a shudder of terror through me. It spikes my determination. 'There must be some way of escape.'

Suddenly she's Kat-Ana again, her eyes blazing with fiery strength. 'My dad was an IT consultant. He said programmers always left a back door in their code. A way in and out. That's what I was looking for in the castle.'

'Any luck?'

'I found a clue scratched on a wall in the dungeon. Don't think it's meant to be part of the game. A message.

'Tween Heaven and Earth lies ESCAPE,
Nearby the Crown seals your fate.

'The only place I haven't looked yet is the Citadel,' she says, pointing to it in the distance, its battlements poking through the clouds. 'That's where the Crown is. But we'll have to fight our way through every VK player.'

'Who dares wins,' I reply, my life-bar now at 100%.

In the distance, a whirring electric hum speeds towards us.

'Time to go,' says Kat-Ana, jumping to her feet. 'That'll be the Skirmishers.'

The Forest

Three gleaming metal droids roar over the hill, their electrified spikes crackling menacingly. They force us off the road and down a narrow track into a forest. We barely make it to the tree line when the Skirmishers suddenly halt their pursuit.

'Stay alert,' says Kat-Ana. 'That means VK players are ahead.'

Trekking deep into the forest, the sunlight

gives way to a gloomy darkness. We enter a clearing. It's eerily quiet.

'A Battle-rena,' whispers Kat-Ana. 'Let's cross before anyone else gets here.'

We're halfway when a shadow drops from the trees.

Drawing her sword, Kat-Ana confronts the tiny black-cloaked assassin. A curl of red hair is clearly visible through his mask.

'Ginger Ninja!' I exclaim, delighted to see our friend.

He stares at me, his eyebrows wrinkling in suspicion.

Then he throws a gleaming star.

Kat-Ana shoves me aside. The metal star strikes a tree trunk behind, then explodes. Burning wood flies everywhere.

'Ginger Ninja. It's us! Scott and Kate!'
I scream as we run for cover.

'He doesn't recognize us,' shouts Kat-Ana,
diving behind a rock.

Another tree bursts into flames above our
heads.

As he throws a third star, more kombatants
enter the Battle-rena. A Special Forces soldier
attacks him from behind. Ginger Ninja
stands no chance.

I dash out to save my friend, driving the
soldier back with a flying kick. Ginger Ninja
thanks me by punching me in the face.

'Don't fight me,' I plead as he unleashes a
series of lightning-fast strikes. I block his
attacks, not daring to retaliate.

'But that's the whole *point* of VK!'
Ginger Ninja replies, landing a devastating

side-kick that sends me flying across the clearing.

I collide with a tree and crumple to the ground. My life-bar flashes 70%.

Just as he's about to follow up with his Killing Strike, a Shaolin warrior monk attacks him. Ginger Ninja disappears in the mayhem of combat.

I feel a hand grab my arm and turn to defend myself.

'Come on!' insists Kat-Ana.

'But what about Ginger Ninja?'

'We can't help him now. He's lost to the game,' says Kat-Ana, cutting a path through the seething mass of fighters. 'We *must* get to the Citadel before the same happens to us!'

The Citadel

'There it is!' exclaims Kat-Ana as we burst out of the forest.

The Citadel hangs in the sky, tethered to the ground by a seemingly endless stone stairway.

The fight out has been bloody and messy. My life-bar hovers below 40%, Kat-Ana's 50%. We share the last of her health packs, but afterwards we're only at two-thirds strength.

Knowing the other kombatants aren't far behind, we sprint up the flight of steps. Halfway to the top, I hear the masonry cracking. Slabs of rock peel away and spiral towards the ground, hundreds of metres below.

'Go! Go! GO!' I urge.

We take the steps two at a time, the staircase collapsing behind us as we run.

The higher we climb, the harder it is to stay ahead of the advancing destruction.

Just metres from the Citadel, the floor beneath Kat-Ana's feet disappears. Screaming, she drops like a stone.

I snatch for her outstretched hand.

Somehow I get a grip. Glad to have my avatar's extra strength, I pull Kat-Ana to safety.

We collapse against the Citadel's entrance, breathless and shaking.

'That was *too* close,' I gasp as we watch the stone stairway reconstruct itself – a deadly VK trap.

'Thank you,' says Kat-Ana, kissing me with relief.

I stare at her, slightly taken aback.

Suddenly realizing what she's done, Kat-Ana blushes.

'It's only a virtual kiss!' she blusters. 'Come on, we've got to keep moving.'

Striding over to the great gate, Kat-Ana shoves it open.

Smiling to myself, I follow her inside.

We enter a huge baronial hall. The final Battle-rena.

Flags line the walls and a blazing VK

emblem hangs over the throne at the other end. A shiny marble floor stretches before us, a vast mosaic map of the world etched into its surface. At the centre upon a glass pedestal rests the gleaming Crown.

'Fame and fortune,' breathes Kat-Ana, suddenly transfixed.

'Forget that!' I say, grabbing her. 'We must escape. Remember the clue.'

She nods slowly. '*'Tween Heaven and Earth lies* ESCAPE.'

I point to a small, unassuming wooden door in the far corner of the room. On the floor is the world map. Above the door, an ornate engraving of a heavenly angel.

The Crown

'It really *is* a back door,' Kat-Ana says in surprise.

I make a move towards it, but am yanked back.

'Another trap!' she warns as a great curving blade shoots past, inches from my face.

Six golden scythes now swing across the hall like massive pendulums of death. Their razor-sharp edges whistle as they slice through the air.

'We'll have to time our crossing perfectly,' says Kat-Ana.

Taking a deep breath, we step out into the Battle-rena. It's hard to gauge when to move as the pendulums keep changing speed and direction.

'Behind you!' I shout.

Kat-Ana rolls out of the way of a lethal blade. I'm driven forwards by the second scythe. Leaping past the next two, I make a dash for the door. I'm almost there when I realize Kat-Ana's still in the middle of the Battle-rena.

Heading for the glass pedestal. Reaching for the Crown.

'No, leave it!' I shout.

'But this is the ultimate prize,' replies Kat-Ana dreamily.

Her eyes are glazed over. She's lost to the game.

Nearby the Crown seals your fate.

'Kate, remember who you are!'

But she's no longer listening.

'*LONDON BRIDGE IS FALLING DOWN, FALLING DOWN . . .*' I sing at the top of my voice, prancing around like a court jester to attract her attention.

The nursery rhyme breaks her trance just in time. That's when I notice the gates to the hall burst open and a muscle-bound boxer stride in.

Destroid has come to claim the Crown.

'Run!' I shout.

But it's too late. Deftly avoiding the blades, Destroid blocks Kate's path.

She tries to skirt round him, but he slams

her with a hook punch. Thrown back against the pedestal, Kate crumples to the floor.

Standing over her unconscious body, Destroid raises his fists for the Killing Strike.

'No!' I scream.

Ignoring the deadly pendulums bearing down on me, I launch myself at him. I land a powerful flying kick. But Destroid barely registers the impact. He blasts past my guard and palm-strikes me in the chest.

My life-bar flashes 60%, pain flaring as I feel a rib break.

I try to fight back, but Destroid is too strong. 50%.

My punches and kicks bounce off him. It's like hitting a brick wall. 45%.

Driven toward the rear wall by his

onslaught, I'm almost sliced by a passing pendulum. He catches me with a punishing uppercut. 30%.

My vision pixelates. I'm on the verge of blacking out. 25%. Destroid prepares to deliver his trademark Skullcrusher.

In a last-ditch attempt, I recall Kat-Ana's training and focus all my brainpower on his every move.

The rippling of his muscles. The clenching of his fists. The deep-throated growl as he brings them down.

Behind him, a scythe slows its lethal swing.

I've entered Trigger Time.

Destroid's fists almost grind to a halt as I move out of their path. Then, selecting my Mega-Punch, I hammer Destroid in the gut.

He staggers backwards in slow-mo. Straight into the path of the pendulum.

The strain of Trigger Time is too much for me and the game speeds back up. Destroid's scream rises in pitch like a jet engine taking off.

Though my win awards me an endorphin boost, I'm still weak. 40%. But I'm glad to see Kate's recovered. She gets back to her feet as two more kombatants enter the Battle-rena.

'Kate! This way!' I urge.

'Kate?' she says, shooting me a confused look. 'I'm the warrior princess, KAT-ANA!'

Drawing her sword, she charges at the new arrivals.

Face-Off

'NO!' I shout, dashing to rescue Kate.

I won't lose her to VK. Not after everything we've been through.

But a kombatant, in a black leather jacket and shades, jumps in front of me.

'Time for our final Face-Off!' he snarls.

'Shark?'

He grins, his avatar's teeth filed into sharp points. 'It's BLAZER to you!'

Clenching his fists, two pulse-blades burst

into life from his knuckles. A high-level Mod.

With the speed of a panther, he slashes at me. The lasers rake across my bare chest, singeing my flesh.

I stagger away, blood pouring from the wounds. 35%.

He comes at me again. I block his thrust, a Blazer passing within a hair's breadth of my face. I retaliate with a front-kick, a hard jab and a spinning backfist that connects with his jaw. Shark grunts in pain as two teeth fly out.

Seizing the advantage, I select my Mega-Punch.

But nothing happens.

I've used my last charge against Destroid.

'Blaze 'n' burn time!' growls Shark,

attacking in a furious blur of pulse-blades and flying kicks.

I duck and weave, narrowly missing a pendulum slicing me in half as I retreat. I look to Kat-Ana for help, but she's engaged in brutal kombat with a Shaolin monk.

My only hope is Trigger Time. But I've never done it twice in the same game. There's a chance I'll Burn Out.

With no other choice, I focus on Shark's every move.

His attacks *still* come fast and furious. He catches me in the head with a roundhouse-kick. 30%.

Dazed as I am, my brain aching under the strain, I desperately try again.

This time, the Battle-rena slows.

I evade Shark's laser fist and launch a knife-hand strike to his neck.

Just as my hand reaches its target, Shark speeds up. A pulse-blade cuts across my arm. I scream out in agony. 20%. He kicks me in the chest and I'm sent spinning into the central pedestal. 15%.

VK compresses back to normal time with a thunderclap of sound and vision.

'Think you're the only one who knows *that* trick!' laughs Shark.

I'm too shocked to move. He's mastered Trigger Time!

The pain in my head now rages like a forest fire as Shark grabs me by the throat. Squeezing his other fist, its pulse-blade burns bright orange as he levels it with my right eye.

I'm going to die – for *real*!

'Don't you . . . want . . . fame and fortune?' I splutter, nodding at the glittering prize.

Glancing up, Shark spots Kat-Ana, bloody but alive, going for the Crown.

'Not before I slice you into shark bait!' he spits, tossing me into the path of a speeding pendulum.

As Shark and the wounded Kat-Ana battle for the ultimate prize, I struggle to my feet.

The blade arcs towards me.

I realize there's only one way to save her.

I dive for the door.

PlayPods

I blink as the Hoody comes off.

Ripping at the Velcro straps, I clamber out.

My body feels bruised and battered, my head throbs.

There's a drip in my arm. I yank it free.

Glancing round, I'm completely disorientated. No longer in the Training Zone, I've been moved to a low-lit warehouse. For a moment, I can't believe my eyes. Rows upon rows of PlayPods stretch into the distance, kids plugged into every one.

There must be thousands of them.

Each pod has a vuescreen displaying their tag, Battle-rena, life-bar, vital signs in real life and their date of entry into the game.

Somehow I have to find Kate. Get her out before Shark kills her.

Hurrying down my row, I look for a date four weeks before mine. As I pass one pod, I catch the sickening smell of burnt hair.

I pray it's not her. I check the vuescreen. Thankfully, the date's too early.

Then I find her PlayPod. She's still battling for the Crown. But her life-bar is at 20%.

I call up the menu. 15%.

Rapidly search for an escape option. 10%.

Her body's convulsing within the pod. 5%.

I find the icon and press ESCAPE. The vuescreen freezes at 1%.

I pull back her Hoody. Her eyes focus on me, seem to spark blue, then fade.

'Scott, *never* forget who you are,' she says, smiling weakly. 'I won't.'

Her head lolls to one side. The PlayPod emits a long, droning beep. Her vital signs zero-out.

I choke back tears. On the street, friends are few and far between. It's survival that matters most. Kate was my first *real* friend.

But I don't get time to grieve.

All of a sudden, the overhead lights come on.

I duck down as two Analysts head towards the pod with the Burn Out inside.

'What a week!' grumbles one. 'Three in a

row. We'll have to promote more kids to Elite Gamer status.'

Passing my empty PlayPod, he shouts, 'Hey, a player's unplugged!'

Then he slams a red emergency button and a klaxon alarm blares out.

I run.

The Greater Good

Weaving between the PlayPods, I head for the nearest exit.

Barging it open, I enter a stairwell and begin to climb. Bounding up two steps at a time, I wish for my avatar's strength. By the sixth flight, I'm gasping for breath. Every door so far's been locked.

I hear voices and footsteps clattering up the stairs.

Forcing myself onwards, I reach the

top floor. To my relief, this door opens.

I burst out on to a roof garden, the cold night air hitting my face.

Streetscreens blaze across the city. A glass dome rises before me, through which I see the orphanage's refectory. I hammer on the glass, desperate to warn the other kombatants of their fate. But no one can hear me above Primetime VK.

The shouts of my pursuers are getting louder.

I dash to the edge of the roof. But the other buildings are too far away. Below in the darkness, an inky strip of the city's river reflects the glow of Streetscreens.

'I wouldn't, if I were you,' advises a silky-smooth voice.

Emerging from his rooftop penthouse,

drink in hand, Vince Power flashes his pearly-white smile at me.

'A waste to lose such an impressive kombatant. How *ever* did you beat Destroid's Skullcrusher?'

I don't answer. Trigger Time must remain a secret.

'You know VK *kills*!' I rage, thinking of Kate.

He shrugs indifferently. 'An unfortunate glitch. Only seems to affect kid players, though.'

'But why don't you fix it?'

'It's not that simple. You kids feed VK2's processing unit. Each mind acts as a super-conductive microchip, powering individual enemy avatars. For some reason your death in the game causes overloading. A Burn Out.'

'You're worse than the devil!' I exclaim.

'I'm *not* evil!' he snaps, his smile evaporating.

'But you're killing kids.'

'I've always believed in the greatest good for the greatest number. VK not only provides entertainment for millions, it's solved many of this world's problems. Reduced crime. Taken kids off the streets. Provided this city's only orphanage. It's even environmentally friendly! For a few to die is a small price to pay.'

'Murder is *never* justified.'

'Yet gamers round the world get a kick out of killing in a virtual game environment,' he counters. 'And besides, some pay more, a lot more, for the privilege of killing for *real*.'

'But it's not *supposed* to be real.'

'Is it *really* that different? The same murderous intent is there, whether someone dies or not.'

I'm stumped by his argument. Like a politician, Vince Power's ready with his answers.

'We could do with a gamer of your calibre,' he says, all smoothness and smiles again. 'Together we might be able to fix the Burn Out issue.'

Two Analysts appear behind Vince, their stern gaze not to be trusted.

'Never,' I reply. 'I'd rather die free on the streets than live like a slave in VK.'

'I'm sorry to hear that,' says Vince, gesturing to the Analysts.

They advance on me. One of them has an electroshock stungun.

I take a last glance over the lip of the roof.

'You'll never survive the fall,' says Vince.

'WHO DARES WINS!' I cry . . . and leap into the darkness.

Log-Off

Vince was wrong.

I did survive.

But now I'm on the run.

With a secret no one believes.

Vince Power *must* be stopped.

If you're reading this, be warned . . .

TO PLAY IS TO DIE!

YOUNG SAMURAI

MORE BLACK-BELT NINJA
MORE BLOCKBUSTER ACTION

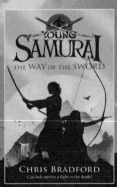

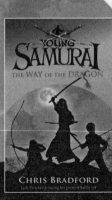

BOOK 4 COMING
AUGUST 2010

Let your training commence at

www.youngsamurai.com